Pearl and Wagner
Four Eyes

Kate McMullan • *pictures by* R. W. Alley

DIAL BOOKS FOR YOUNG READERS
an imprint of Penguin Group (USA) Inc.

*For the Wilson girls: Sadie Louise, Miller Kate,
and Josephine*
—K.M.

*To Mrs. Huntington, who took an interest in
my drawing once I got glasses*
—R.W.A.

DIAL BOOKS FOR YOUNG READERS ★ A division of Penguin Young Readers Group ★ Published by The Penguin Group ★ Penguin Group (USA) Inc., 375 Hudson Street, New York, NY 10014, U.S.A. ★ Penguin Group (Canada), 90 Eglinton Avenue East, Suite 700, ★ Toronto, Ontario, Canada M4P 2Y3 (a division of Pearson Penguin Canada Inc.) ★ Penguin Books Ltd, 80 Strand, London WC2R 0RL, England ★ Penguin Ireland, 25 St. Stephen's Green, Dublin 2, Ireland (a division of Penguin Books Ltd) ★ Penguin Group (Australia), 250 Camberwell Road, Camberwell, ★ Victoria 3124, Australia (a division of Pearson Australia Group Pty Ltd) ★ Penguin Books India Pvt Ltd, 11 Community Centre, Panchsheel Park, New Delhi - 110 017, India ★ Penguin Group (NZ), 67 Apollo Drive, Rosedale, North Shore 0632, New Zealand (a division of Pearson New Zealand Ltd) ★ Penguin Books (South Africa) (Pty) Ltd, 24 Sturdee Avenue, Rosebank, Johannesburg 2196, South Africa ★ Penguin Books Ltd, Registered Offices: 80 Strand, London WC2R 0RL, England

*The art was created using pen and ink, watercolor,
and a few colored pencils on Strathmore Bristol.*

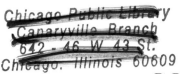
CONTENTS

CHAPTER ONE

RAW BIRD PIZZA

On Monday morning, Nurse Nice

came into Ms. Star's classroom.

She wrote on the board: Eye Test Today.

Wagner squinted and read,

"Eye . . . Toast . . . Toady."

"Uh-oh," said Pearl.

Nurse Nice put tape on the floor.

She hung a chart on the wall.

"Line up for your eye test!" she said.

Pearl was first in line.

Wagner was right behind her.

Last in line was Ms. Star.

"Cover your right eye and read

from the top," said Nurse Nice.

Pearl covered her eye.

"G W V G S B E," she read.

"Left eye," said Nurse Nice.

"Keep going."

"N O I H W," read Pearl.

"Your eyes are fine," said Nurse Nice.

"J H E R L C," Pearl read quickly.

"N O S Z L E P H U L Y T H."

"Next!" said Nurse Nice.

Nurse Nice flipped the chart over.

"Cover your right eye and read

from the top," she said.

Wagner covered his eye.

"E," he read. "B? No, wait. P!"

"Left eye," said Nurse Nice.

10

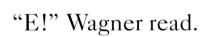

"E!" Wagner read.

He blinked.

"E . . ." he read again.

He shut his eyes

and shouted, "E I E I O!"

After the eye test,

Nurse Nice gave Wagner a note

to take home.

"You need to see an eye doctor," she said.

"Who, me?" said Wagner.

At recess, Lulu said,

"Do you have to get glasses, Wag?"

"No way," said Wagner.

Pearl pointed across the street.

"Read the red sign," she said.

Wagner squinted.

"Raw Bird Pizza," he read.

"Glasses time!" said Pearl.

CHAPTER TWO
Wagner's New Look

Pearl and Wagner walked

home from school together.

"I wish *I* needed glasses," said Pearl.

"Glasses can give you a whole new look."

They passed Ron & Bert's Pizza.

Next to it was Gayle's Glasses Shop.

Pearl pointed to a pair of glasses

in the window.

"If I wore these glasses,

I'd look like a rock star!" she said.

"You think so?" asked Wagner.

Pearl pointed to another pair.

"In these, I'd look like a scientist,"
said Pearl.

"Right," said Wagner. "A mad scientist."

"These would make me look like

an actor," said Pearl.

"Pearl—starring in *Swamp Monster*!"

said Wagner.

"Cut it out!" said Pearl.

"Sorry," said Wagner.

"But you don't even need glasses."

"Oh, right," Pearl said.

Pearl studied the glasses again.

"Don't worry, Wag," she said.

"I will find a great new look for you."

"I like my old look," said Wagner.

"I am never getting glasses.

Never, never, never!"

The next Monday morning,

Wagner waited for Pearl on the corner.

"What's wrong?" said Pearl

when she saw him.

"I got glasses," said Wagner.

"Put them on!" Pearl said.

"No," said Wagner. "I hate my glasses.

They pinch my nose.

They poke the backs of my ears.

They make me look like a guppy."

"Let *me* put them on!" said Pearl.

"You asked for it," said Wagner.

He took the glasses out of his

backpack and gave them to Pearl.

"Everything is fuzzy," said Pearl.

She tried to walk.

"I feel dizzy! And sick!"

She turned to Wagner.

"But how do I look?" she asked.

Wagner squinted at Pearl.

"Blurry," he said.

Pearl gave Wagner his glasses back.

"Put them on, Wag," she said.

"I will tell you how you look."

Wagner put on his glasses.

Pearl gasped.

"You look so cool," she said.

"I do?" said Wagner.

"You do," said Pearl. "Come on!

Let's show Lulu and Bud and Henry."

She grabbed his arm and

they ran to school.

CHAPTER THREE

FOUR-EYES PIZZA

When they reached the playground,

Pearl called, "Wagner got glasses!"

Everybody ran over to see.

"You look great," said Lulu.

"You look smart," said Bud.

"You look like
Wagner with glasses,"
said Henry.

"Thanks," said Wagner.

Just then two big boys

came over to Wagner.

One boy said, "Hi, Four Eyes!"

The other boy laughed

as they walked off.

"Phooey!" said Wagner.

"Now I am Four Eyes!"

He whipped off his glasses

and threw them into his backpack.

"I have on a hat," said Henry.

"I guess that makes me Two Heads."

"I'm wearing boots," said Bud.

"That makes me Four Feet."

Wagner smiled.

"I have on a scarf," said Lulu.

"I'm Two Necks!"

Pearl waggled her gloves and said,

"Twenty Fingers!"

Wagner put his glasses back on.

"The name's Four Eyes," he said.

The bell rang and they all

ran into the classroom.

Ms. Star was writing on the board.

"Pizza Party Today!" read Wagner.

"Hooray!" said Bud.

"Why are we having a party?"
asked Pearl.

"To celebrate seeing," said Ms. Star.
She turned around.

Everybody gasped.

"Wow!" said Pearl.

"You look like Ms. Rock Star!"

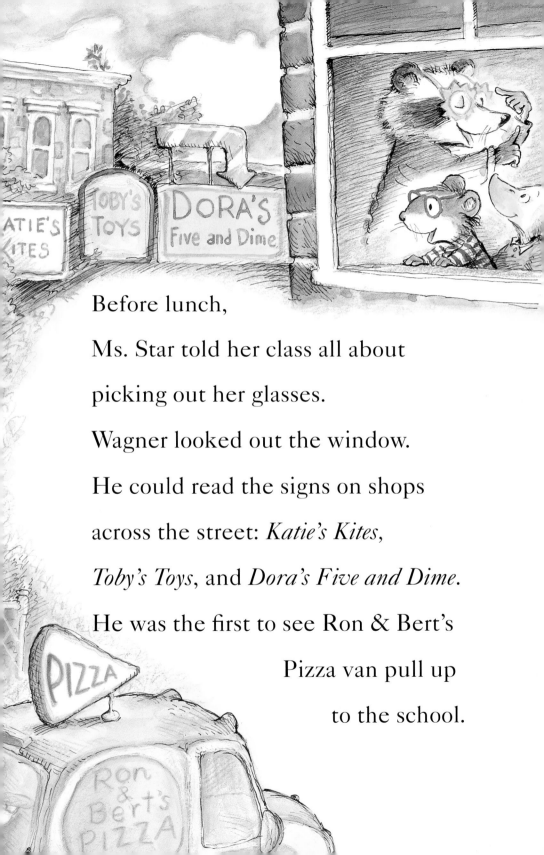

Before lunch,

Ms. Star told her class all about

picking out her glasses.

Wagner looked out the window.

He could read the signs on shops

across the street: *Katie's Kites,*

Toby's Toys, and *Dora's Five and Dime.*

He was the first to see Ron & Bert's

Pizza van pull up

to the school.

Everyone pushed the desks together
to make a table.

Ms. Star covered the table with
a red-checkered cloth.

"I ordered a special pizza," she said.

"Close your eyes!"

"Now . . . open!" said Ms. Star.

The pizza had pepperoni and olive eyes.

It had glasses made of

green pepper strips.

And a big red pepper smile.

"All right!" said Wagner. "Four-Eyes
   Pizza!"
"Eat up!" said Ms. Star.
   And everybody did.

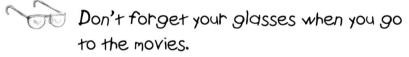 Don't forget your glasses when you go to the movies.

When your glasses get so smudgy you can't see, it's time to clean them.

 Keep your glasses in a special place where they will be easy to find.

Don't put your glasses down on the ground where they could get stepped on.

Keep your glasses away from babies and animals.

If you sleep with your glasses on, they can get lost in your covers.

 Keep a glasses case in your backpack—just in case.

 You will look cool in your *new* glasses and all your friends will want to try them on!

earpiece

arm

bridge

frame

nosepiece

lens

case

cleaning cloth

cleaning spray